The Art & Practice of
Creative Visualization

The Art & Practice of
Creative Visualization

Ophiel

WEISER BOOKS
Boston, MA/York Beach, ME

Revised edition published in 1997 by
Red Wheel/Weiser, LLC
P. O. Box 612
York Beach, ME 03910-0612

Library of Congress Cataloging-in-Publication Data

Ophiel.
      Art & Practice of creative visualization / Ophiel
          p. cm.
      Rev. ed. of: The art & practice of getting material things
  through creative visualization. 1967.
      Includes index.
      ISBN 1-57863-001-0 (pbk : alk. paper)
      1. Imagery (Psychology). 2. Visualization. 3. Creative
  ability. I. Ophiel. Art & practice of getting material things
  through creative visualization. II. Title.
  BF367.O65   1997
  133.3'2—dc21   96-51424

Typeset in Benguiat

Printed in the United States of America
BJ

09 08 07 06 05 04 03 02 01
10 9 8 7 6 5 4 3 2

I dedicate this book to all those who are endeavoring to better themselves, mentally, physically, and materially through the study, practice, and application of the occult.

I hope you will acquire the knowledge and understanding to use the material offered in this book. And, through its successful practice, I hope you attain the happiness you desire.

Contents

A MESSAGE
FROM OPHIEL

(Publisher's Note: Ophiel died in 1988 and although this message is dated, and Ophiel can't answer reader's questions, we left the introductory material as he would have presented it.)

Without doubt the greatest mystery on Earth is the mystery of our physical existence. We are stuck here, and what do we know about why we are here? And what can we do about it?

There are some who say "they" know what physical existence is all about and some people listen to and follow "them," hanging on "their" every word and gesture; believing everything "they" say completely.

Fortunately it happens that I have a defect(?) in my character, which probably comes from my Capricorn birth sign, because Capricorn is ruled by

Saturn, the tester. I wish quite often that I didn't have this defect(?). For then I could live in peace, in a fool's paradise like the others!

This defect consists of not being about to accept self-styled prophets' sayings and teachings without raising the following awkward question: Is what they say true? And the test is: Does what they say work, and produce results? And if what they say does not work, then it is not true, and into the garbage with it!

But out of all these years of turmoil and search has come something for you! I have found that people—all people—have certain definite powers. Powers of which they are often not aware of having and powers that seem almost divine!

Henceforth your objective in life should be the discovery and development of your personal powers, for your use and benefit, to bring you happiness, and enlightenment, and illumination.

I wrote this book to bring to you definite workable knowledge about one of your powers—the power of creative visualization.

If you will stop, analyze, examine, and consider, you must find that our physical existence consists almost wholly of "things" coming into our personal-life-physical-existence-surroundings. These physical incoming things are of two types or kinds. The first type is mental-emotional-circumstantial-events; and the other type is material. As students, you should be deeply interested in the *modus operandi* of your powers of mental-visualization-creation-creating, and all its ramifications. You should also think about how the development of these powers pertains to your personal life—with an emphasis on the idea of conquering physical matter by learning to control it, as well as bringing into your personal possession the material things that seem to be so necessary now for your happiness and physical-plane-well-being.

Do not be afraid to do this. Attempts at creative-visualization are nothing new in human evolutionary development. Untold ages of times ago, your cave-man-ancestors secured needed-desired-circumstances-things by various types of creative visualization combined, of course, with endless kinds of devices, both physical and mental, to assist in the creative visualization work.

As you know, your stone age ancestor's creative visualization consisted of picture-drawings on the walls of caves—pictures showing them successfully hunting game and successfully defending themselves against enemies; and these creative visualizations must have worked, also successfully, because our ancestors did survive, and we are here today as a result of their survival! A modern application of the cave wall pictures will be given in this book. For your own advancement and understanding I ask you to study carefully this ancient application of this magic art, and the modern one, and make the connection in your own thinking.

Also for untold ages human beings have engaged in asking the supposed higher powers for the favorable circumstances wanted or needed. These higher powers were supposed to be "outside" of us. There are powers "outside" of us, but I cannot go into the question of these outside powers, called God or Gods, in this book. All I want to do in this book is to direct your attention to your latent powers, those powers that you possess now. I will repeat—you, all of you, possess powers, which, if used properly—are able to handle the creation of circumstances favorable to your physical being. One of these powers is the power of creative visualization:

Do not worry about not learning to use the laws of these powers perfectly. If you learn the laws, and use them, as well as you can, they will work, maybe a little slower, but they will work. Do remember that all the things that you have now, things that you do not want, you brought to yourself by the unconscious use of these laws, and you did not special practice on that did you?

Also have no fear about using the laws. These laws, the embodiment of your powers, are as much a part of you as your life is. There is nothing wrong in using them. The only wrong is in not using them and allowing physical life to hurt you.

Now go to it. Make your life the life you want. Go—Go—Go.

CHAPTER 1

THE ART AND PRACTICE OF CREATIVE VISUALIZATION

Millions of human beings suffer from the "slings and arrows of outrageous fortune," not knowing that we each possess many powers which, if used properly, could enable us to control our material physical existence to a large extent, and relieve ourselves of a lot of trouble. One of the unknown, unused powers, we possess is the power of creative visualization.

Creative visualization is the name for a magical operation wherein we create in our "mind's eye," or in our imagination, the idea-image of something, or some circumstance, or some circumstances we fancy would be of benefit to our physical life comfort and add to our physical well being. This well being is usually called happiness.

Upon the successful completion-creation of such an image, the mental imagination image will become real and will enter our daily life.

Many books have been published describing this magical process. Creative visualization has been called by various names, but all names mean the same thing. It has been called "contacting God for your daily supply," or "creating opulence through esoteric work," or "consciously creating circumstances," or "Seven Steps," as it is called in one school. This book is another book about a creative visualization system.

However, it is my intention to go much deeper into this subject of creative visualization. I intend to give you all the knowledge and information necessary to enable you to understand, use, and practice successfully the great art of creative visualization.

And I do this with the sincere hope that you will be able to use this great art so well that you will be as happy as it is possible for you to be.

Before we go any further into a study of a system of creative visualization I think we should stop and ask first a big question: Can and does a system of creative visualization really work? And if, for now, we assume that the answer is "Yes," then some other questions are in order. Questions such as: How does it work? Does it work for big things, or does it work for little things only? What is the reasonable truth about it?

We can start our consideration, of the idea, of the existence of such a thing, as a system of creative visualization, by giving some weight to an old proverb: "Where there is smoke, there is fire." On the one hand, in our material life on this earth, we usually find that if an idea exists, even a crude superstitious idea, there is always some kind of a truth behind it.

Therefore we might think that if a system of mental creative visualization had absolutely nothing behind it, the idea of such a possibility would not even exist.

Of course, on the other hand, there's other old proverb: "If wishes were horses, beggars would ride." This gives some weight to the contrary idea that visualization systems don't work. If such a simple process—merely visualize what you want and it comes to you—would work easily, then there is a snag! If this idea worked, there would be no poor people in the world at all, nor any unhappiness if happiness depended upon a material supply of PHYSICAL THINGS that we could just visualize and get. Apparently creative visualization systems "work" for some people and do not "work" for others. If a visualization system does work, it will, apparently, work at certain times, and, apparently, not work at other times! Again a visualization system will work for some people instantly, and for other people, it never works at all! It could be truthfully said that systems of creative visualization appear to be a hit or miss proposition that cannot be depended upon for constant results, especially on the physical plane, where results must be expected and must work out properly.

After much study and experience, I believe I am in a position to understand the creative visualization process. The art of creative visualization depends for its successful operation upon correct knowledge, correct understanding, and rigid following of definite rules!

To be a little more specific, the art of creative visualization, and all other esoteric work, involves work done on other kinds of planes—the inner planes—in addition to the work done on this physical plane! And inner plane work requires knowledge and practice based on that knowledge, and more practice, and more practice.

In creative visualization work, we use all the planes involved in our cosmic existence; the etheric, the lower astral, the higher astral, the mental plane, and the causal plane. All these planes have definite rules and laws from which they will not deviate one iota.

The rules of all these planes must be followed closely if you are to expect good, final, physical-plane end results from inner plane operations. Even when these laws are followed closely, intelligently, and correctly, there can be other local and cosmic conditions which can prevent these secret techniques from working temporarily. Some of these will be noted later in this book.

I am going to list a number of inner plane laws. I intend to treat each of these laws in the order of its importance, and as completely as I can. Then I will set up the operational technique for each law as completely as I can. Please pay close attention to each law, technique, and practice as it is introduced here. Make a very strong attempt to understand and master each in turn. Your individual mastery of these laws, and their practices, will constitute your final mastery of the great art of creative visualization and prepare you to master other esoteric laws.

The following laws govern the art of creative visualization. I will devote a section to each of these laws. The object of this study will be to change the law into a personal technique, for your use. Make the best effort you can to master these laws. Never give up. In the event you do not succeed in practicing these techniques as perfectly as a master would practice them, it would mean only that it will take you a little longer to accomplish desired results.

A brief description of each of these laws and an outline of some details of its method of study are shown in Table 1 on page 6.

Law Number 1—The Law of Physical Visualization. For creative visualization to be successful the operator must mentally create a visible mental PICTURE of the thing, or the circumstance, wanted. This kind of Mental Visual Creation is not easily done by the average person. Unless this mental creation is done, creative visualization work cannot proceed to a successful conclusion.

Law Number 2—The Technique of Physical Visualization. The technique-law is described and directions are given for carrying it out. Most of the laws are described in this first section. The practices are described in the latter part of the book, but in this case the practices are given immediately after the description of the technique. I do this so that you will have some work to do while you are studying the rest of the laws. That is, I give one kind of practice and the rest of the practices pertaining to other symbols are given in the latter part of the book.

Table 1.   The Laws.

Number	Name of Law	How Studied
1.	The Law of Physical Visualization.	Discussed and described.
2.	The Technique of Physical Visualization.	Practice with physical objects.
3.	The Technique of making physical visualization objects— connected with Laws 1 and 2.	Study and practice.
4.	The Law of the Sphere of Availability.	Study.
5.	The Law of Limitation.	Study.
6.	The Law of Binding.	Study.
7.	The Law of the Barrier.	Study.
8.	The Law of the Treasure Chart.	Study.
9.	The Law of E-Motions.	Study.
10.	The Law of Reversal of Planes.	Study.
11.	Summary and Practices.	Study.

Law Number 3—Continuation of the first two laws with more detailed directions for making symbols for visualization practice and some additional instructions.

Law Number 4—The Law of the Sphere of Availability. This law is one of the most important factors in the magical operation of creative visualization. To my knowledge this law has never been taught before. The lack of knowledge of this law is the cause of all the failures attached to trying to use the art of creative visualization. The practices of this law will be found in the latter part of this book in connection with the case histories.

Law Number 5—The Law of Limitation. This is another important law. If you don't know about this law, it prevents the working of creative visualization art but somewhat less than some of the other laws. I do not mean to imply that I discovered these laws or that they have never been published before. These laws existed, but their direct connection to magical occult work had never been established as clearly as they are now. Also, the practice of the Law of Limitation will be explained in the latter part of this book in connection with case histories, as will all the rest of these practices.

Law Number 6—The Law of Binding. This is another unknown law that greatly affects creative visualization. Understanding this law, and working with it, can greatly assist you.

Law Number 7—The Law of the Barrier. This law governs the art of changing words into emotions and emotions into words. Attempting to work creative visualization with words alone, or emotions alone, is a difficult process. Understanding this law can make your work more effective.

Law Number 8—The Law of the Treasure Chart. A treasure chart or map, as it is also called, is a visual aid to creative visualization work. A correctly made treasure chart is of tremendous value in creative visualization work. Full directions follow for making this magical tool.

Law Number 9—The Law of E-Motions. The part that emotions play in creative visualization work is usually referred to very seldom. A full explanation follows so you will understand the part emotions play in life and you can take full advantage of them.

Law Number 10—The Law of the Reversal of Planes. Ordinary words are not very good when it comes to explaining the finite metaphysical operations of inner being "things." Thus the fact that all planes are reversed to each other is almost unknown to many occultists. And this reversal also becomes reversed at times! The lack of knowledge of planes reversal is another reason why ordinary creative visualization work fails.

Summaries are mostly given through case histories.

•   •   •

At the beginning of this book I said, "endless books have been written describing a secret process called creative visualization," and then I said, "This book is another one of those books about creative visualization systems." Now imagine that you are asking natural questions and I am giving the answers.

The first natural question you would ask is: "If there are so many other books on this subject already written, why then another book?" And the correct answer to that question is, "Yes, there are lots of books already written on this subject, but the instructions contained in those books do not always work so well or, let us say, do not work so well as to preclude the introduction of another book on this subject."

And your next natural question would be, "If the instructions given in those other books did not work so well then how did the authors get away with writing books that contained instructions that did not work?" And the correct answer is: "Those instructions, as given in those books, did work!! *But only for the authors of those books!*

What these questions and answers add up to is this: due to a peculiar personality quirk, which these authors alone automatically, naturally, possessed, *these authors unconsciously did all the techniques of the creative visualization work properly and thus the process works for them successfully!*

Once these authors get a creative system working for themselves they hasten to write a book about it. Then esoteric students hasten to buy the book to get the magic system to work for them. And the magic system works sometimes, and sometimes it doesn't, depending on how closely the student is like the author.

It never seems to occur to those authors that their processes might not work for others as it did for them. They publish their personal, empirical system of creative visualization and not a word is said about *the principles upon which their system is based.* In fact, their working of creative visualization might be so natural to them that they don't even know about any basic principles. It is strange, but there are people like that in the world. These people do things right the first time they try, without any previous training at all.

However I was never one of those kinds of people. I had to learn how to do things by learning the basic principles, and then work them through. I cannot learn any other way. (If you are one of the natural workers, then you are lucky!)

So now I will repeat myself again and say that the laws governing the art of creative visualization are listed in this book; and each of them will be explained in detail, and the basic principles of these laws will be laid out for you to understand. Then, through understanding, you will be able to adapt these laws to your personal uses and needs. Use them. The existence of principles, techniques, and rules which can be learned shows that this work of creative visualization is an art. Many of us can become masters of this art.

Mastery of the art of creative visualization is a big step toward the mastery of the art of life. As a matter of fact, you are using creative visualization every second of your life! None of us are very successful in living and having the kind of life we would like to have. Yet everything we do have, that we do not want, and which makes us very unhappy, *we created ourselves, for ourselves, and by ourselves, by our own mental powers!*

Naturally we did this creating ignorantly, but we did it nevertheless. As I said before, the time can come (and I hope this book will hasten it for you) that you can take, and will take, your own personal Divine Powers into your own hands and direct the right use of this power. Then you will begin to use your divine powers as they should be used, and as you should use them—in the right way and for your own benefit!

What does using your powers for your own benefit mean?

Basically it means that we all use our basic creative powers every second of our lives. But we use these creative powers wrongly. What does "using our creative Powers wrongly" mean?

The most outstanding thing it means is using our creative powers ignorantly. Our present use of our creative powers is like giving a baby a gallon of nitroglycerine to play with!

Another misuse of our creative powers is the spasmodical use of these powers. We don't have a definite idea of what we want to do, or to be, or to have. There are other endless misuses of our powers but these two are enough to throw a monkey wrench into the best life in the world.

How to handle your powers properly is the subject of this book, and will be explained as we go on. For now, all I want you to know is that there are two things necessary for the successful use of this creative art, and they are: 1) the knowledge that you have great creative powers; and 2) the knowledge that you have heretofore used these powers ignorantly, and hence wrongly, all your life but now you are to learn to use these powers correctly. So now, knowing that the successful use of the process of creative visualization is possible to all of us, in some degree, through the right uses of basic principles, we can go on from there.

CHAPTER 2

LAWS GOVERNING CREATIVE VISUALIZATION

The first reason why the creative visualization process does not work perfectly (as it should work) for the average student is implied in the title of this book: *Creative Visualization*. Half of the creative visualization process consists of a procedure called visualization. Now exactly what is visualization?

A glance into the dictionary gives the following definition: to make or to become visible, especially to see or to form a mental image of; the natural ability to be able to form a clear mental image of something in your mind-memory. This is an ability that not every person possesses. Certainly this is an ability that varies with different people and varies widely even with those who possess the ability naturally.

Here then is one of the main reasons why this mental creative visualization process does not, and cannot work, for all people, as it should. An ability to create clear, mental, picture images in the mind, is required; and not all people possess this image creation facility naturally. I did not have this facility myself, and I had to work hard to get it in enough degree to get positive results from my creative visualization work. I have no doubt that those authors who have written books about creative visualization possessed those creative visualization mental image-making abilities naturally, and it probably never occurred to them that others did not have that ability in the same degree that they had it.* If they did not think that everyone possessed the same ability as they did, then I am at a complete loss to account for the fact that these people did not work with exercises to develop this ability in their students. One thing I can say for certain is that in the books I read on this subject not one of them provided any of the exercises that I am going to give to you. This work will enable you to develop your visualization ability as much as is needed for your creative work.

In the beginning of my esoteric studies I was not able to proceed in this art until I developed the following exercises. Practice with these exercises enabled me to learn to create clear mental images of the physical things I needed or desired, and I

---

* I want to call your attention again to the strange omission in practical exercises on developing mental images made by the previous teachers of this art. Obviously, as the art succeeded with them, they just assumed that all other people had this ability. The lack of a positive image-making facility is one of the most potent factors in the failure of this kind of creative work. How can you possibly succeed in this work if you cannot visualize?

can tell you that when my mental creations were clean cut and clear, then my creative visualization succeeded.

Now that I have emphasized the importance of physical visualization, I will give you some work to do. (It was my intention to explain all the laws one by one and then give the practices in the use of the laws in the latter part of the book. I will do this with the other laws, but I will give you this visualization work now, so you will have something to work on while you are learning the rest of the laws.)

The visualization practice, in connection with this first part of the mental-physical-creative-visualization, will be a magical ritual. In this magical ritual you will use a great deal of mental-imagination in connection with physical actions. You will first learn to "work" the ritual physically and then "work" it mentally, visualizing it as you work it. Finally you will 1) first work it physically; 2) then work it mentally; 3) then work it both physically and mentally at the same time.

This is the first part of the practice visualization to develop this faculty in you. The second part of the process will consist of work with symbols, which you will find at the end of the book and on the inside front and back covers. You will also find directions for making your own symbols and coloring them. In the advanced part of this work you should make up your own symbols anyhow.

Start your first work in the following manner:

The first work is a very seemingly simple little ritual. If you make a big mistake that will hold up your magical proficiently for a long time, just imag-ine, as I did, that because this ritual is so simple, it does not amount to very much, and so neglect to learn and do it. This simple ritual is very helpful and very powerful. Learn it and use it all the time:

Memorize the following material and memorize it so well that you will be able to recite it easily without stopping to think of what comes next. The ritual sounds easy, and it is easy, but it is also a bit complicated for it involves some movement and word-actions. If you continue in esoteric study, and you should, you will eventually understand the meanings of the words and actions, but for now, work the ritual as it stands. It will still work.

1) Touch the forehead and say ATOR (Thou Art);
2) Touch the lower breast and say MAL-KUTH (The Kingdom);
3) Touch the right shoulder and say VE-GEVURAH (and the Power);
4) Touch the left shoulder and say VE-GEDULAH (and the Glory);
5) Clasping the hand and fingers together before the breast say LE-OLAHM (for-ever AMEN).

This ritual exercise is the preamble to the next sec-tion which is as follows. Stand in the center of as large a room as you can find to work in. Face East. Visualize a steel dagger in your right hand. Now here is your first work to do. Find a picture of a dag-ger, or find a real dagger, or borrow one, or do something to get yourself a real dagger model to visualize. Then concentrate on your model until you can recall the image of it to mind easily.

The carefulness and the accuracy of your work in setting up this, and the other models for visualization purposes, is the degree of magical accuracy you will attain in your magical work.

"Hold" your imagined dagger in your right hand and trace, in the air in front of you, a large star according to the outline shown in figure 1. Trace the star accordingly as it is day (morning), or evening (night). Practice making these stars many times until you can trace the star without any jerky motions. You can practice making some stars on a piece of paper. Keep the proportions of the star good. "Draw" the star, making your movements deliberately and slowly.

After you have perfected making these star movements, add the following material to the ritual. Take 1 tablespoonful of rubbing alcohol or whiskey and place it in a saucer. Light the liquid

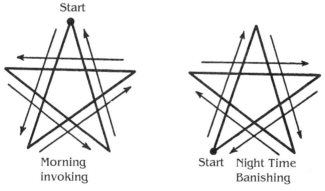

Morning
invoking

Start   Night Time
Banishing

Figure 1

and note carefully the blue color of the flame. (Don't waste the whiskey or burn the house down!) Get this blue color flame fixed in your mind. Also remember the way the flame wavers. Practice until you can visualize the color and wavering and recall them to memory perfectly.

Now you can proceed with the main ritual. Face East. "Take" your steel-image-dagger in your right hand, and visualize the dagger outlined in the wavering blue flame. Make a pentagram star, according to the time of the day, and visualize the star outlined in the blue flame. Then pronounce the name Y H V H (YOD-HEH-VAV-HEH).

Now "see" through the center of the large flames an outlined star and a beautiful dawn! Pink to rosy clouds. The East is the quarter of air, so feel air. Imagine, and feel, a cool soft breeze coming from the dawn clouds and passing over and through you, and through you again and again. The name of this East Wind is Eurus. So call it by this name.

When you have turned South, make the star and then pronounce the name ADNI (AH-DOH-NAI). Through the center of this South star, "see" the following scene. A tropical island. Warm blue sea waters dashing on coral reefs. Beyond the coral reefs lie long white beaches, and beyond the beaches palm trees sway gently in the hot tropical wind. Feel this hot wind pouring from the center of the star into you and warming you through and through. The name of this south wind is Notus. So name him and call him.

When you are finished with the South, erase it gently from your mind and continue to make the blue fire circle around to the West. There make your blue flame star and pronounce the name AHIH (EH-HE-YEH). Visualize a waterfall tumbling down over a cliff and dashing on the rocks at your feet, sending up a cloud of mist and spray. Feel this misty spray on your face like a gentle rain. Feel wetness and coolness through and through. The name of this West wind is Zephyrus, so name it and call this name.

When you are through with the quarter of the West, continue, with your flame dagger, the circle around to the quarter of the North; trace the fire-flame star and pronounce AGLA (AH-GAL-LAH). The North is the quarter of the earth element. These quarters have no relation to the usual material ideas of air, fire, water, and earth, but are concerned only with the qualities of these elements. Hence North, the quarter of earth, is not the North Pole of the Earth but is North, the quarter of earth. It is in the North quarter of earth that all the other elemental forces end. I will repeat this: All "forces" coming through to the "outer" from the "inner" end in the North quarter of the earth. Therefore earth is the great end storehouse of all forces, and these forces are all things! You will find in earth all the things that you are looking for, the things that you need to make you happy.

So, therefore, when you visualize the quarter of earth, through the blue flame star, you first visualize, before you, vast fields of ripened grain and vast fields of ripened corn and other cereals. Beyond these fields are vast orchards of fruit trees loaded with all kinds of fruits. Beyond the orchards stretch great areas of grasses on which graze great herds of animals. Beyond the herds start forests of trees and beyond the forests are mountains.

And these mountains are full of minerals that we use in our daily lives, and the mountain tops are covered with snow and ice. The melting of this snow and ice makes an abundance of water which flows down to nourish the living, growing things below. All is peace and plenty, full of all the things you need to make a full and happy life for yourself. The name of the North wind is Borus, so name it and call this name.

When you have finished working with the quarter of the North, continue the flame circle on around to the East, and end it there, where you started. You should then be completely surrounded by a circle of blue flames with a blue star at each quarter.

Close the ritual by repeating the Cabalistic Cross exercise followed by these words and actions. You are facing East. Throw out your arms in the shape of a Cross and say:

> Before me is Raphael;
> Behind me is Gabriel;
> On my right hand is Michael;
> And on my left hand is Auriel;
> Before me flames the Pentagram and
> behind me shines the six-rayed star.

The above ritual constitutes the first part of the practice in connection with learning physical and mental visualization.

CHAPTER 3

THE SPHERE OF AVAILABILITY

We now come to the law listed as number 4 on our list. I have named this law **The Sphere of Availability**. This name designates one of the most important occult laws ever given. All the work you will ever do now, or in the future, along the lines of creative-visualization hangs on the knowledge-theory-base of **The Sphere of Availability**.

Now I sure hate to keep on saying, "Give this next subject your utmost attention, etc." But in this case, it is more true than otherwise, and a lack of knowledge of the Sphere of Availability is fatal when it comes to accomplishing anything through creative visualization. The one big reason why mental visualizations fail to "come true," or do not reach physical consummation, is a failure to know about, understand, and allow for the existence of the Law of the Sphere of Availability. Once this law is clearly understood, it explains why some students' visualizations succeed easily while other students' visualizations never succeed, no matter what they do, or how hard they visualize. In the examples that follow, look for the ones where creative visualization work was done naturally.

For the technique I am about to explain to you (as you have no doubt guessed by now) I have coined the name The Sphere of Availability (I did this coining of names even after I complained about others doing it, so I feel guilty!*)

The concept of the law is so subtle that I have decided the best way to teach an understanding of this law is by means of case histories. I will now give a number of case histories about people who have succeeded in creative visualization work and then point out the correct use of the law in these cases.

I am going to tell the very first story I ever heard about creative visualization work. The following is from a book written by a Mr. Richard Ingalese. Mr. Ingalese was a lecturer and occult teacher in this country at the turn of the century. He apparently died in Los Angeles about 1930 as near as I can find out. He and his wife wrote some books about esoteric study and these books are still quite good for beginners in this line, although they are a little outdated now.

In one of his books, Mr. Ingalese—talking about the Law of Opulence which was his name

---

* I feel that I should mention here that it was my repeated failure to achieve success with visualization that led to my discovery of the law of The Sphere of Availability.

for creative visualization—tells a story about a young man who lived in Paris many years ago. This young man came from a family of rag pickers. That is, he made a living by picking over the piles of Paris rubbish and salvaging anything usable; but from what I know of the French, and their thrifty habits, I would say that the pickings were slim, indeed.

This young man attracted the attention of a person who was versed in the secret traditions, and this person decided to help the young man. He gave the young man a manuscript and told him to practice the knowledge contained therein. And this the young man did. The manuscript contained directions explaining the art of creative visualization, or, as it was called in the manuscript, getting things through thinking.

After studying the manuscript, the young man decided he would attempt to practice the great art. (The following is very important.)

The young man decided, for his first visualization attempt, that the first thing he really needed was a small piece of carpet to put beside his bed to protect his feet from the cold stone floor when he got out of bed in the mornings. He proceeded to visualize for a piece of carpet and in a short course of time a woman gave him a piece of carpet!

This simple demonstration so convinced him of the value and power of the art of creative visualization that he proceeded to practice it for the rest of his life, and when he passed on he had many hundreds of thousands of francs, and francs were francs in those days.

We will now consider a case that I know about personally. Many years ago I lived in La Jolla, California, and I used to attend a little Theosophical meeting that was held each week. As is somewhat common in Theosophical circles, the people who attended came from different backgrounds and had many different kinds of ideas about the esoteric study.

I recall one lady who was active in semi-esoteric work. She used to teach, in some kind of a WPA group in San Diego, how to make Treasure Charts (as we will study later) such as are taught by the Unity people in their work. She adapted her own ideas to these Treasure Charts and then taught them as a kind of creative visualization system of her own to a mixed group of people in her classes.

The people in the class, having nothing better to do for the moment, used the idea in jest, and one man made up a chart for a bottle of whiskey, while another made a chart for a beautiful woman!

It turned out that shortly afterward, someone gave one man a bottle of whiskey and the other was introduced to a beautiful woman! The two men were so frightened by these happenings that they fled the classes and refused to have anything more to do with this stuff!

At one time I owned a small rooming house that I had gone to a lot of trouble to fix up very nicely. I did not seem to be able to get any income out of it. I made up a chart and decided that I would be satisfied with a certain income per month for the time being and I soon had it!

At another time, I needed a small hand punch for some work that I was doing but I was not able to buy one. I did some visualization work for a punch (frankly, without much hope, as I was new to the game). A few days later, I was accosted by a drunken man who offered me a punch for a small sum of money. I did not like the idea of the man being drunk and selling something for less than it was worth, so I refused to buy the punch, whereupon the man threw the punch down at my feet and stalked off in high dudgeon! You certainly could not ask for more of a miracle than that!

I am not sure where I heard the next story; I don't think I read it anywhere. So if I am using anyone else's story I apologize in advance. A lady saw, in a large department store, a very beautiful hat that she decided she wanted. She could not afford the hat, so she decided to get it through creative visualization. In order to get the creative visualization picture correct in her mind, she went into the store and, leaving her old hat on the counter, put on the desired hat and went to a mirror to see how she looked. She wanted to get the visualization picture absolutely correct in her mind. When she was through viewing the hat, she returned to the counter and, looking about, could not find her old hat! After searching for a time she called a clerk who called the department manager, and learned that another clerk had sold her old hat! The manager said she could have any hat she wanted in the department, so she walked out of the store with the hat she wanted and visualized for!

What is the most outstanding feature of these stories? What is the one thing they all had in common? Other than the obvious fact that they all got what they wanted through a visualization process, is not the hidden fact that the desired thing was within the normal reasonable reach of the person? Shall we say that all these things were "gotten" by these people within their normal sphere of availability?

These people did not ask for Rolls Royces, mansions, huge bags of gold, or the Moon with a fence around it. No! The things they asked for were a small piece of carpet, a bottle of whiskey, a beautiful woman, a hand punch, a woman's hat. Things that are there now.

My research has convinced me that the main reason why visualizations do not work for us all the time, as we want them to work, is that we ask amiss. That is, we do not get the things we want, not because God does not want us to have them, but because those things are not in our sphere of availability at the time.

The truths of divine metaphysics are so grand, and divine, and sound so right, that new students, hearing and reading about them for the first time, are greatly tempted to throw caution, and reason, out the window and imagine that they can work miracles easily, especially after reading a few pages of a creative visualization book.

New students then proceed to visualize for large things. Big things. Valuable things. Things that are far beyond their ability—not to visualize-imagine-desire, but far beyond their present ability to demonstrate. And all this is especially so if these new students have champagne appetites with a beer income. A champagne appetite and a beer income is no joke to those who have it.

To reinforce your understanding of the law of The Sphere of Availability, I am going back to the story of the young French rag picker to compare his story with another story I will give.

You will recall that the first thing the young rag picker visualized for was a piece of carpet to protect his feet from the cold stone floor in the mornings. This young man had nothing, but absolutely nothing. (In his case having nothing was a great blessing.) He did not have something that he could have traded for a carpet. He did not have a little money so he could have bought himself a piece of carpet—he had nothing.

So therefore, having no resources at all, he was able to decide on the piece of carpet as what he needed and wanted most, and he concentrated on the creative visualization for this piece of carpet. And as the carpet came to him soon, through his work, it proved, among other things, that the carpet was within his sphere of availability.

Now I will tell you another story. It concerns a man who had a positive genius for running large department stores. He had a terrific ability to sell goods and to manage efficiently such a business. He was employed in a very large store, but not in the top capacity. The store was family run, so the top jobs were held by family men who were content to use our man's ability without giving him the appropriate title and salary.

Under these circumstances, this man was not able to move into the position he wanted, no matter how much he tried to get ahead where he was. He came into contact with a metaphysical worker whom he allowed to do some work for him, and through this metaphysical work, the man secured a position in one of the largest stores in the world, where he was soon at the very top spot and made a terrific success of everything he touched.

Now I want you to think: do these two cases have anything in common, and, if so, what is it? At first there seems to be no connection between these two cases, but a closer look shows that they have one very important thing in common. Both people had the things desired, or were ready for the thing desired, or creatively visualized for, in their sphere of availability.

Please read this several times: The things the two men desired and which were creatively visualized for—one doing the work himself and the other having it done for him, but meaning the same thing—those two different things were in their sphere of availability.

In order to make absolutely clear what I am driving at, let us assume that the young rag picker, instead of visualizing for a piece of carpet, visualized for the top manager's job of the largest department store in Paris! Now, although everything taught about creative visualization is true, and the work is very powerful to bring us what we visualize for, common sense (the law of the physical plane) will tell you that the young man would not get the job easily, or if he did get it, he could not hold it.

Again, no matter how powerful the magical creative visualization work was, the fact remains that he is, was not, fitted for the job! For this reason, and this reason only, the job is definitely not within his sphere of availability.

It would not be the creative visualization work that would be at fault, but the complete lack of common sense, and the complete lack of obedience to the laws of the physical plane. If the young man was not fitted for the job, he could not do the work, even if the creative visualization forces brought him the job.

Or, to put it another way, we can say truthfully that before creative visualization work can bring a job successfully, a tremendous amount of work would have to have been done to prepare for the successful holding of such a job. This kind of work would take no end of time, no matter how you look at it. Mr. Ingalese speaks of people who visualized for things beyond their present sphere of availability and did not get the things until their next reincarnation on earth; and at that time they did not want the former things anymore, but wanted something entirely different, and so life went on in a vicious circle.

So now you can ask another natural question: "How did the creative visualization process work for the young man so that he became so rich?"

Very important. Study the following very hard. What happened in his case was, as said before, that the first successful demonstration so encouraged him and convinced him of the workability of creative visualization powers that he determined to practice this art for the rest of his life. The next thing he did was to select another object he needed or wanted, which happened to be in his Sphere of Availability, and when that thing was demonstrated, he went on to another and still another. *Each successful demonstration added something material to his life, and thus enlarged his Sphere of Availability.*

As the Sphere of Availability enlarged in size, other things formerly not possible became possible, or, as should be said, the Sphere of Availability increased in size until formerly impossible things became easily available and were on hand almost automatically. For heavens sake, and your sake, read this over until you understand it completely and absolutely.

The following subject is so important that I am going to risk boring you to tears and repeat it, some of it, in another slightly different form. Please absorb it and successfully use it for your benefit.

To sum up the foregoing case history: the young rag picker, having no money or resources at all, and having decided to practice the art of creative visualization, picked out, with good common sense, an article he needed—a piece of carpet.

The young man did not do creative visualization work for a palace, or for a million francs, or for a yacht, or for any of those things that people sometimes try for the first time they use the creative visualization process. (Oh yes, we are all guilty of this sort of thing.) All the young man asked for was a simple thing that he really needed. A palace, for example, was not needed, and because this thing he needed was within his Sphere of Availability he got it in a relatively short time.*

The second step the young rag picker took is equally important. He did not, upon completion of his first successful demonstration, jump to palaces and millions of francs, or other big things. He proceeded to select another object that he needed for his immediate comfort and well being, and proceeded to demonstrate for that thing.

Mr. Ingalese does not tell, in his book, what the next article actually was, but I am assuming, from the nature of the first article selected, that it was something simple and necessary, and very probably of the same nature as the piece of carpet. The young man continued this process for the rest of his life, and his life became a process of gradual growth and acquirement: *the possibilities of further acquirement increasing with each new asset acquired.*

Now what about you and I, and our use of creative visualization? We should have a reasonable belief that the system does work, if for no other reason than we use it wrongly all the time. Now we want to use it right, so how do we, you and I, go about using it?

---

* Our lives are so constituted so there is a big difference between what we really need now and what we would like to have or dream of having. Our lives are like a puzzle of many pieces that we must fit together ourselves, and only we can work out our lives. You must start to build up your life a piece at a time, you must decide what piece is to be next fitted into your pattern. You can dream about other things, but the first work you do should be for what you need next.

Let us go back to the rag picker. Now I do not want to use this system to get a piece of carpet. I do not need a piece of carpet. I do not need to use this system to get a piece of carpet. I have lots of pieces of carpet about me now. I have some extra money available so I can buy many pieces of carpet if I want them. So pieces of carpet are not my problem as it was to the rag picker.

However, while I do have some things now, I am not completely satisfied with what I now possess, and I do want to use this system of creative visualization to get the things-circumstances-situations-possessions that I would like to have, or do want, or think I want.

On the other hand, from what I learned about the Sphere of Availability, I do know that many of the big things I would like to have are not in my Sphere of Availability, let's face it, at this time. Also let us face the fact that we are dealing with definite planes of manifestation, each of which has definite laws, and each law of each plane must be obeyed. There is, in addition, the law of the last plane, the physical plane of matter, and that plane is very hard to move, to understand, and to operate on.

What should I do, and what must I do—and what you must do, too—in order to make the creative visualization process work for us? Clearly it would seem that the very first thing we "middle class" (whatever that is) people must do is to discover exactly where we stand and where we are in regard to what we want on the physical plane. We have to pinpoint our exact position and know where we stand exactly. We must find exactly the things we want and find out exactly where they are in regard to our Sphere of Availability. We must find out exactly what things are missing in our lives and how these things stand in relation to our Sphere of Availability.

To sum this up: the intelligent and accurate appraisal of your present life's position in regard to your wants, needs, and desires is the first step in the right use of creative visualization. The second step is the accurate appraisal and understanding of these things in relation to your Sphere of Availability.

It can be said, quite truthfully, that we middle class people are the most difficult subjects for creative visualization work. We have many things on hand now and many other things automatically coming to us. If we should start creative visualizations for something that is automatically coming to us, it would be a waste of time and effort. In all esoteric work you have to look out for a situation wherein you use these powers to accomplish something that could be accomplished in another, more natural, way. For example, by using ordinary planning you might find that you could trade something you no longer want for something you do want and need. To have done otherwise than this natural method would have been a waste of the art of creative visualization, and a waste of time and effort.

We must use common sense and think about what we should work for. We must consider the state of growth we are in, and the state of growth our Sphere of Availability is in. Few people will demand too much of a beginner. So don't demand too much of yourself in the early stages of your

work. Later on, when you have achieved some success you will guide yourself by the development of
your Sphere of Availability. What is wrong with at-
taining your goal in several easy steps instead of
one big hard jump?

I will refer again to Mr. Ingalese and his book.
Mr. Ingalese is the only teacher I have ever found
that taught, in connection with creative visualization, a system of gradual growth. He called his idea
creating a "center" from which to draw the things
you want and need. Every other teacher that I read
always strongly stressed the idea that in your visualization work, under no circumstance, must or
should you designate from what source your desired things should come. That idea never did ap-
peal to me because I am a natural planner, and I
like to know at all times where I stand, and what I
am doing.

Mr. Ingalese tells a story about a woman who
built up a center gradually. She is supposed to have
come to San Francisco a long time ago. In some
way, not explained in the story, this woman acquired
a facility in the art of creative visualization and used
it from the start to BUILD UP A GRADUAL GROWTH
CENTER. She first got a job by visualizing it. Then
she got several promotions in the same place. Then
she visualized herself going into metaphysical work,
and after that she visualized herself receiving com-
pensation worthy of the effort she spent doing work
for others, and someone gave her a large sum of
money in gratitude for work she did, etc.

I will admit that this story does not follow the
pattern as laid out by many other teachers, but it

seems to me that this system of gradual growth is far more sensible than doing a lot of general visualizing without any idea of anything definite and not knowing if the thing desired is in your Sphere of Availability or not.

I will also admit that you should not, for example, concentrate thoughts on some person with the idea of forcing the person to give you a chunk of money. Nor does it seem sensible to concentrate on getting things that belong to other people. Nor should you visualize your rich uncle being dead so that you could have his money, etc. I really believe that these are the sort of things other teachers were thinking of when they said you should not designate where the visualized objects should come from.

It would seem rather foolish today to designate where your supply should come from because there are so many ways in existence and more are coming every day. And again it would be silly to want the same things others have. There is nothing that cannot be improved: why should you want someone's car when a newer model would be better?

So I cannot find anything basically wrong with building up a center of supply, according to approved visualization methods, as long as you leave the channels open so things can flow into your center of supply from what source they may. I would suggest that you do not picture yourself doing work in exchange for things as you might find yourself working more than you would like. You can start out by doing some kind of work, but you should shift your pattern quickly to doing work that you know you will like to do.*

For God's sake combine inner spiritual knowledge with earthly common sense. The two are needed to make a good whole.

The creative visualization mental operation is a true magical operation. True magical operations are things that are not too well known and understood. I learned these things through my own work; after years of striving, and meditation, and study, I can give them freely because I am under obligation to no one. Therefore I am able to give you secret knowledge and teachings. For Heaven's sake, use it.

---

* I regret to have to warn students that if you have gotten so far down the Sphere of Possession that you are in actual physical want for food, shelter, and the necessities of life, this process of creative visualization is not for you now. It would take a student of terrific powers to instantly create the things you need, and a beginner in this art could not do it—this process is too slow for that, even under the best of circumstances. In the case of such dire physical necessity, trying to use this process of creative visualization would be like trying to grow a tree in a flood to get wood to make a boat to escape the flood. I wish I did not have to say this, but you must make allowances for the physical plane. If the arrival of this book finds you in dire need, you must be sensible and accept government aid for immediate assistance. That step taken, then turn to Christian Science, or to Unity practitioners, for immediate help. They have been in the work for many years, and can help you until you can help yourself. When your immediate needs are taken care of, then come back to this book and work to make sure you never get into such a state again.

CHAPTER 4

THE TECHNIQUE OF LIMITATION

One of the main parts of a true magical operation is called "The limiting of the Object of the Operation." What does this mean? Magical operations, involving as they do the forces of the inner planes, deal only with forces. Inner plane forces are subject to inner plane laws, and are certainly not subject to physical plane laws. This fact practically everyone knows, of course, but few people realize the implications of this fact.

Basically, when you deal with inner plane forces you are dealing with forces that have no confinement of any kind. Two inner plane forces occupy a single space at the same time. Inner plane forces fly off in all directions at once. Time, as we know it, is not the same for them. Both start and finish at the same time—beginning and ending at once. (Now do you see why it sometimes says in the Bible

I am the Alpha and the Omega, the beginning and the end?) And yet in order to obtain your outer desired-physical-plane-end-results you have to work with inner plane forces first. To handle these inner plane forces you must know something about their nature and how to "work" them.

Dion Fortune did say something about this, but did not explain the full implications. You have much to learn and I will give it to you in time, and as we go along, but for the present all you have to know is: at the start of any magical operation a limit must be set to designate the extent of what you want to accomplish in that particular operation. Unless you do this, you are going to have trouble getting the forces to make the transition from the plane of force to the plane of form, and to stay there.

You are able, by means of ordinary mental magical daily operations, to contact and gather forces together quickly, but unless the gathered forces are quickly conducted into a "form" here on this physical plane, they will fly off as fast as they are gathered.*

Now appears two of those seemingly endless factors that influence creative visualization work, and I trust that you are not going to blow up at their endless appearances. We will come to an end of them sometime, surely at the end of this book! It is the lack of knowledge about these things that makes our work so futile when it comes to helping ourselves through magical work.

---

* The object you desire in your visualization work is the FORM that limits the forces that your work gathers.

Well, we might as well get it over with—one of these factors is something that you could call "too much of a good thing."

To state it briefly and quickly—it is a Law of the Inner Planes that once you have succeeded in getting an inner plane force to work for you, or to "flow" into your life, this force has a tendency to keep on flowing-working. And this flowing-working will keep up long after you, or any other operator, has achieved the original objective of the original starting of the flowing-working! I note an apparent contradiction in the above and what I said before, but there is none, really. I told you that inner plane forces do not operate the same as physical plane forces. It is true that inner plane forces can be gathered together quickly, and they do, and they can fly away as quickly. But with long persistence, and other unconscious magic techniques, you can succeed in getting the forces to flow for you, and then they keep on flowing!! (Consider "flow" the same as "work") This automatic overflow can cause as much trouble and disappointment in results as no flow at all. The simplest form of trouble that this over-flow can cause is to create a condition of tension in you after you have received the original thing you visualized for. In this tension you are vaguely dissatisfied with the whole creative visualized matter-operation, and you feel that you want to go on demonstrating the same thing-object over and over.

And the other factor is that many people do yield to that continual flowing-in pressure, and go on accumulating the objects, first wanted, beyond all reasonable need of them. This happens to people who were once very poor, or in great need of money. Because a mental, natural, and personal creative visualization system was developed, money started coming to them, but, having set no limit to their objective (at least for this one visualization creation) the incoming flow, once started, kept on coming, and, in the end, the incoming flow took over their lives and they continued to do nothing but get money. All their other objectives in life were lost sight of, and some of these people actually starved to death because they could not control the incoming flow of money—to divert some of it to spending patterns. *They were gripped by the power of the forces they had set in motion.* They could not spend the money for what they originally wanted it for—a good time to be had in life.

In the paper, this morning, was the story of a woman who dropped dead on a San Francisco street, of starvation, and over one thousand dollars was found on her person by the police! Another example of this sort of thing is *The Christmas Carol* by Charles Dickens. Ebenezer Scrooge turned to making money because of a great love disappointment in his life, and he felt he needed money to make up for what he lost. Scrooge, having once gotten a flow of money started his way, was not able to control it thereafter, and amassing money took over his life to the exclusion of all else.

This concludes the theoretical discussion of The Law of Limitation. I will now give a few directions to guide you in practice, and will give more detailed directions in the latter part of the book.

So, for the time being, what has to be done to make your creative visualization work come out right? The first thing to do is to figure out exactly what object, or thing, or circumstance(s) you want to bring about, or acquire, by creative visualization practices.

Having made this decision, you then write out, in exact detail, a description of the object or circumstance desired, and state clearly that this is all that you want from this one operation. Make the end of the operation as clear as the beginning.

As an example, let us assume that you are working for a piece of carpet as the Paris rag picker was. You would write on your paper exactly what you want and what you want it for. You can also add a description of how you expect the carpet to be used and how you expect it to "feel" in use (this part is important; more of this later). Now conclude your writing by pronouncing a statement such as, "and for the purposes of limiting the effects of this operation, I hereby state that the sole physical desired result of this operation is this piece of carpet, and also for a psychic result I expect a deep satisfaction from the use of this piece of carpet!

CHAPTER 5

THE LAW OF BINDING

In magical operations of all kinds there are always two kinds of forces involved. Actually, any kind of an operation—any action of any kind—physical or inner plane magical—involves two kinds of forces. To say it another way, to make it as clear as possible, any and every force in our physical cosmos is really a double acting force. Every force is dual in nature, and always has been dual, and could exist in no other form than dual. There is not a thing in the physical universe that does not have two sides to it. Even God has two sides.

We use both sides of everything and we have completely lost sight of the "other side" of the things we use. Do you ever stop to think that every time you cover yourself with a blanket that you are using one side only and that there is another side to the blanket? Could the blanket exist without the other side,

the side you do not use? (This is not too good an illustration, but it will do to enable you to think about
it, and to keep the concept as simple as possible.)

Here is a different illustration. Do you realize
that every time you drive your car forward, you are
exerting an equal force backward? If you will study
some physics about the Laws of Motion, you will
find this is true.

So again I say, when we use a physical-plane
force we do not use just one side of the force, or
only one aspect of the force, but we use both sides
of the force at once. As in the simple illustration of
the blanket and the more complex operation of the
automobile, we must use both aspects of a force or
we can't use it at all. In fact, a force could not exist,
even on the inner planes, if it did not have two
sides to it.

However when using inner plane forces to accomplish something on the physical plane we want
to use only one aspect of the force, and not both
aspects. There is a reason for this. One aspect of a
force will bring a thing to us, and the other aspect
of a force will take it away! Or to say it in another
way—a force can bring something to us and the
same force can take it away!

It follows naturally that if we want a certain
thing, the aspect of the force we want is the aspect
that will bring the thing to us!

Therefore it is imperative in all magic works,
and in all kinds of other works, that you must recognize the existence of the other side of the force
that you are invoking. Remember, when you con-

tact a force, you contact both sides of it at once, and at the same time, and both sides have equal power. It is the lack of knowledge about this "secret" fact that causes so much trouble in the magical workings of would-be magicians. Either your magical operation works like mad (I mean literally) or does not work at all.

Therefore, when you want to use a force to accomplish a certain kind of work, you must use the "side" of the force that you need to accomplish the work that you want to do, be it constructive or destructive, and bind the other side of the force that you are using so it will not function in the operation you are performing!

If you do not bind up the one side of the force that you are using (the side that you do not want to operate), then in any particular operation you perform you will invoke-contact both sides of the force at once, and they will nicely cancel each other out. Or, to enable you to understand it better, I will put it in a little different way. When you start a magical operation without a binding, you can, and often do, use the aspect of the force that you want to use; but as time goes on, the one-sided use will create a strain, or pressure, and this pressure will, sooner or later, bring the opposing force, now concentrated by the removed dilution of its balancing opposite, back into operation with the results, harmless enough when said this way, of completely neutralizing all the previously done work and bringing back all conditions, physical and otherwise, to the same condition prevailing before the magical work was started. To say it another way, it makes a hash out of the whole thing.*

If you will look carefully, you will see this cycle repeated time and time again in the history of nations in the world as far back as you care to go. You can see it operating in our daily lives every day in all our little disappointments and breakdowns in daily living.

So now that you know about the Law of Binding, what must you do to make your magical operations come out right?

The operation of mental magic you will be doing by using the art of creative visualization, as given in this book—to set a limit on the extent of each operation you perform—will have the same effect as binding the opposite force.

If the work you are attempting to do does not involve too great a dislocation of your surroundings, if your sphere of availability is ready to supply you with what you are working for, setting a sensible limit on the size of the operations you are conducting will be sufficient for all normal purposes. If you are creatively visualizing for something really big, or if you are attempting real magical work, it will be absolutely necessary to bind the opposing dual force.

---

* A way to see this quick reversal in action is to watch the people at race track. A man will win a large sum of money which was done by successfully invoking pressure on inner plane forces. Even if it was done ignorantly, the power of the Will, even of an ignorant man, is very great (at times). And then a few minutes later the man will lose all that he won. The force gave and the force took away.

I suggest that you confine yourself to the type of specialized operations that I have given you so far; go one step at a time and gain what you want slowly. I can tell you truly that if you get too large a thing by these creative visualization methods, unless you protect yourself by binding, you are apt to lose it all again when the reaction takes place. *Build up your life by the slower, more careful, well thought out methods I have given you, one step at a time, and you can expect to hold on to your gains, increase them, and use them in the right way.* Gaining a thing through creative visualization (not too large a thing as to cause the dislocation as aforesaid) and starting to use the thing is another form of binding.

CHAPTER 6

THE LAW OF
THE BARRIER

In this section I am introducing a new subject—the law which pertains to the art of creative visualization. I have not found this law in this exact form before. I have named this seventh law of creative visualization The Law of the Barrier. An understanding of this law will enable you to work the art of creative visualization a little more perfectly.

In the use of the art of creative visualization methods to get what you want, much confusion exists regarding the use of words as opposed to symbols and pictures. There appears to be two schools of thought about the use of words versus picture symbols, and neither of the two schools seems to know too much about it conclusively.

In the past thirty years of esoteric study I ran across first one school of thought and then the other school. They seemed to run in cycles. First there would be schools and books dealing with words, mantras, chants, etc. And then there would be schools dealing with mental visualizations, pictures, etc. Certainly you have all heard of Coué and his, "Day by day I am getting better and better." No, it is, "Day by day, in every way, I am getting better and better." Also you must have heard of Eastern Mantras. Chants, and fairy tales are full of words like en-chant-ment (en-in, chant-sing, ment-state of), and In-voking (In-in, voke-voice speaking). All these things pertain to word-sounds. It appears that "states" have to be gotten by words, and "things" have to be gotten by mental pictures. It probably could be said that the East is interested in "states" while the West is interested in "things." Therefore I presume the choice is up to you. If you want "things" then follow the instructions as given in this book, and if you want "states," then follow the Eastern type of instructions, or work out your own system of the knowledge you have been given here.

Speech, in the sense that we use word sounds to convey ideas to each other, is, in the evolutionary existence of human beings, a recent invention. In thinking of speech you must never confuse human speech with the speaking of god, as, for example, where in the scriptures it says, "God spoke." The speech of god is an entirely different thing from human vocal sounds. But as this is the only kind of speech we know about, we are apt to mistake the one for the other. The creative speech of the divinity is connected with the Tattva Akasha "sound granules." Sound granules are vibrations, and these vibrations shape the astral light—the logos—into all things, and then change these things to material things by an entirely different process.

Thus, this human speech of ours, due to its recent invention, does not pertain to the depth of our being, our inner subconscious mind, but rather speech pertains to our outer conscious mind only. (You should know from your studies that you have two minds, an inner one and an outer one; the outer one called the conscious mind and the inner one called the subconscious mind.)

The existence of these two minds in you is what makes all the trouble in the world. Or, maybe I should say that the separation of these two minds makes all the trouble for you in the world. *

Attend to the following knowledge carefully. Words (speech) are the "language" of the conscious mind, whereas feelings are the "language" of the subconscious mind.

So I repeat again: all the trouble we have in the world, in living this material life successfully and fully, comes from the differences in communications between the two minds: from our inability to get these two minds to talk to each other—to get ideas and commands over to each other! Conscious-you has to learn to talk to unconscious-you! In most of our lives we seldom ever tell ourselves what we really mean! We need to.

---

* For those of you who are "ready" for "higher things," I will drop a big fat juicy hint as to what Illumination really is—becoming a Master, becoming an Adept, BECOMING LIKE A GOD, means the two minds fuse into one! Enough said!

By studying this material, and learning the art of creative visualization, you are entering upon a new phase in your life; a phase in which you can learn to communicate properly to and with your subconscious mind. You can learn to give your subconscious mind positive directions and have them obeyed by it in order to get things done for you.

At this point, I will part with a couple of big secrets. Big secrets you would never get except from some secret society, and then only under big oaths of much secrecy; and you would never be able to use them for your own benefit or tell them to other people so that they can help themselves. Oh Heavens! Again, for heavens sake, use these secrets for your benefit, and then for the benefit of others.

First big secret! Your inner you is connected almost directly with the inner forces of the physical cosmos!!!

And the second big secret! The inner forces of physical cosmos are the emotions-feelings of God!

The word e-motion means moving (something moving). Movements on the inner planes are vibrations of different kinds and of different forms. These inner plane vibrations, as soon as they come in contact with your inner plane subconsciousness, become "visible" to you as your emotions!

And the converse is also much more importantly true to you, your subconsciousness emotions—generated by you—reach out and contact these inner plane forces, and influence them to your benefit!

Now, with this imperfect and incomplete explanation of the basic foundation of this creative visualization art out of the way, we can proceed. The reason I use the words imperfect and incomplete is that modesty forbids me to claim, as others do, that I have given you the whole truth and whole truth of be-ing. All I have given you is enough the-ory-knowledge to enable you to proceed with your work in this art.

The art of creative visualization would be a ter-rifically simple matter if we could just "talk" our de-sired visualizations into physical existence. But that simple thing we cannot do. You could spend a life-time talking about what you want, and still not get one word through to the submind. Talking: words must be linked with EMOTIONAL FEELINGS IN OR-DER TO WORK! Yet we cannot THINK, or even oper-ate-communicate, on the physical plane without the use of words, and it is by WORDS that the OUTER HAS TO COMMUNICATE WITH THE INNER.

However I am glad to be able to show you that through all these contradictions between words and emotions, and emotions and words, there is a path that does go right through it all. To explain this path, I have invented a name for it (a practice I ab-horred when others did it and here I am doing it again). The name I have invented is The Barrier!

Imagine a "place" inside your mental being where there exists a sort of "fence." This fence, or barrier, separates your outer being from your inner being; it separates your conscious mind from your subconscious mind. You, your conscious mind, is outside the barrier and YOU, your subconscious mind, is inside the barrier. (This is not too good a way of explaining it, but this explanation is only to describe a theory so your mind can have something to grapple with. Don't demand too much from a theory; as soon as you get used to the idea, you will not use the conception anyhow.)

Imagine that the *barrier* works in the following manner: words come up to the barrier, strike the barrier, sink in the barrier, and then emerge on the other side, the inner side, as emotions!

Conversely, imagine emotions coming up to the inside of the barrier, hitting the barrier, sinking into the barrier, and emerging on the outer side as words!

When you can visualize this operation, you have made a great advance in the mastery of the esoteric arts.

This theory of The Barrier may be only an invention of my mind to help you understand these important operations; but you can see for yourself that something like this must be so in order to seal off your Inner Being from your Outer Being. If this barrier did not exist, the least little word would raise a perfect hell of emotions that could not be controlled. If the barrier did not exist, the least little emotion would raise a storm of words that would be meaningless to you and all others.

The barrier slows down both of these transfer actions and allows proper living to proceed in a halfway orderly manner. Understanding the instructions in the barrier process enables you to deliberately control the barrier actions, going and coming, or as might be said—to control the traffic both ways. You can now consciously link your words with emotions and your emotions with words.

CHAPTER 7

THE LAW OF THE TREASURE CHART

The next Law we will study now is called The Law of the Treasure Chart. We will also consider another tool which can be used in your creative visualization work. This Treasure Chart tool is a rather well-known device, being an application of some very old magical principles. I have reason to believe that the pictures and decorations on Egyptian tombs were early treasure charts. As soon as a royal child was born in Egypt, a tomb was immediately started for him or her. On the walls of the tombs were painted pictures of his or her life up to his or her death, and this was done while he or she was still an infant. These pictures show the child as having all the good things in life right up to death and even beyond that! The pictures show male children winning all the wars and capturing large numbers of prisoners. In other words, a wonderful life was set up in advance.

These pictures were painted on the walls of the tomb and made alive, and powerful, by the magic of the priests. In all cases, unless the priests withdrew their magic protection, these pictures preserved the child throughout the life, and the child lived this protected path during physical life.

At the present time I find that the Unity people are using this magic tool in their work. It seems a little strange to find Unity people using this magic device, as none of their other teachings have any connection with magic that I can find, for they use mostly metaphysical, mental teachings. But, be that as it may, we can be thankful that the magical tool still exists, and that its use is open to us all. (I just called the Unity office in this city and the lady there tells me that the Treasure Charts are still used in their work only she called them Treasure Maps. If you feel so inclined, get some of their magazines and see what additional things they have to say about the technique of this magical tool. Perhaps you will find additional data that I do not give, which will help you in your work of getting the most out of a Treasure Chart. If it works for the Unity people, it should work for you, as you will be using additional magical techniques that they do not use.)

You will recall that earlier I told you about a lady in La Jolla who had taught this Treasure Chart system. One of her students made up a chart for a beautiful woman, and another student made up a chart for a bottle of whiskey, and both got what they wanted, and it scared the wits out of them. (These students were far more sensible in their askings than many students who ask for the Moon with a fence around it the first time they use a creative visualization technique.)

The technique of preparing and using a Treasure Chart is basically rather simple. The first thing to do is to get a large sheet of paper or cardboard, or some other large surface on which you can fasten things say, 15″ × 15″ or larger. The "surface" of your chart should be kept in as private a place as possible. The chart should not be in a location where others can view your chart freely; and you should show it to others very sparingly, if at all, and then only to those who are in complete sympathy with your aims in life. A man and wife might make a chart together for their mutual benefit, but that is about the only exception to this secret rule. So let your chart be private and hidden.

After you have selected your chart surface and mounted it somewhere away from prying eyes, the first thing to do is to place a boundary line along the edges of the chart. Why? Your answer is, "to invoke the Law of Limitation," of course. I think at this point I will add some more material.

As students of esoterica, you should have some knowledge about the planes. The inner planes are treated somewhat more fully in my book, *The Art and Practice of Astral Projection.* In that book you are shown how to enter the inner planes and become familiar with them first hand. But until you are familiar with the inner planes you will have to take my word for it. (I respectfully suggest that if you do not have the book that you get a copy and study it thoroughly. There is also much ordinary material in there which you will use in your esoteric work and studies for the rest of your life. All my books are written for one purpose only, and that purpose is to help you help yourself.)

So, placing a border-boundary line on your chart's surface not only places a physical boundary line on your physical chart's surface, but it also places an astral boundary line on the astral plane counterpart of the chart. Everything on the physical plane has a counterpart on the inner planes, way up to the top of Creation. Now do you see why you should place a boundary limitation on your work? For example, I am told that the designs of a rug are all duplicated on the astral plane, and it seems logical that they would if the idea of counterparts is true. In Oriental countries, where these things are automatically known or sensed, when a rug is designed and woven, breaks are left in the pattern of the rug so any elementals who happened to get into the astral pattern can escape from the design of the rug!! (That is all I know about it. Why the elementals cannot get out of the design sideways is beyond my understanding. I have heard that they can move only in a straight line. Doesn't make much sense in the absence of positive knowledge. Maybe they are dumb, as I have also heard.)

Anyhow, placing a boundary line on your chart will limit the boundary of your operations, by placing a boundary on the counterparts of the pictures that you put on the chart to express your desires. Remember your desire pictures are attached to the real physical object/things on the inner planes, and this attachment is the basic-why-reason your chart will work, and can be used to bring you the things you desire.

After the foregoing preparations are finished, you can then start your search for desire-representing-pictures and material to place on the chart. What you are to look for, and look everywhere for, are pictures that embody your desires.

Where do you find these pictures? Naturally, in our modern world, you will find these pictures in magazines, sales pamphlets, brochures, illustrated books, and other similar things. It is fortunate, for our search, that every well sought after desired thing in this life is represented by some kind of a magazine to the "trade."

For example, if the things you desire are some special kind of thing, then find the trade magazine for the thing you desire. Let us say, for example, that you are interested in horses. You would secure the trade magazines for horse owners, and in those magazines you would find pictures of horses which would embody your desires. What I want to emphasize here now is that IT IS THE SEARCH, AND RE-SEARCH, THAT YOU DO TO FIND PICTURES OF YOUR BASIC DESIRE-OBJECTS THAT ASSISTS GREATLY IN INFLUENCING YOUR SUBMIND TO START THE INNER PLANE FORCES TO WORK TO BRING ABOUT YOUR DESIRES. When you find a picture or illustration that gives you a thrill, arouses desire in you, then clip it out and fasten it to your chart. Fasten these pictures to the chart with Scotch tape. Use your own personality-imagination-desires-ideas-emotions, and everything basically you, to make your chart.

Here are a few basic directions you can use on your chart. If you feel like using any of these ideas, you can do so, but if you don't feel like it, then do as you please. You can place, at the top of the chart, a picture of something inspirational, and place a picture of something that expresses thanks at the bottom of the chart. You might say that big things should go to the top of the chart and smaller things near the bottom. You might consider the bottom of the chart as nearest the present time and the top of the chart as farthest away from the present. You might consider the left side of the chart as where things might come from and the right side as the things already arrived or near arrival. If you don't like any of these ideas, then follow your own ideas, as what you feel might be right for you in a special way.

Select pictures of the things you desire and place them on the chart accordingly. Do remember the sphere of availability. Also keep in the background of your mind the other creative visualization laws that you have learned.

Now, in the case of the Treasure Chart, it won't hurt to put pictures of fine things, pictures of cars, jewels, fine homes and estates, so you can have something to look at, and admire, and arouse your emotional desires for better things, and to develop your taste for better things, and to get in the habit of thinking of the best things at all times.

Thinking of the best things in the world is not going to hurt you as long as you see these things in the correct perspective. Call this section your dream section, or a dreamboat, or anything like that, as long as you do understand what it is. Remember that all the finest things in the world can come to you, but they have to come through the laws of the physical plane, usually in exchange for money. One thing is certain: these things have to come to you through an increased sphere of availability, but you have to give this increased sphere of availability a chance to grow. You have to give it time to build up.

I have found that everybody sets up this chart differently, and this is the reason I am giving you so much leeway to follow your own personality in these instructions. The main idea is to search out pictures of the objects you desire. Hunting and searching for these embodied desires stirs your inner being to activity, and it is the constant reviewing of these pictures afterward that reinforces and steps up inner plane activities to bring you the things you want.

View the chart every day. In a few weeks, you should be able to recall the images to memory very easily. Once you recall these pictures, you should be able to manipulate them about to suit yourself.

Referring again to *The Art and Practice of Astral Projection*, the last section is called "The Symbol Method of Projection." After you have studied this section, I call your attention to the fact that you can use this same projection method to project yourself into these pictures on your Treasure Chart. You will find this a curious and rewarding experience. This type of projection can be of great assistance to you in stirring your inner being into greater activity in getting you what you want.

After you learn how to bring material things to you, you will be able to also bring other changes; you can learn to heal yourself, and to look at the world differently.

CHAPTER 8

THE LAW OF E-MOTION

The word "emotion" comes from the same root as the word "moving." An e-motion is alive. The truth is that there seems to be evidence that an emotion is actually a part of your being—the real you.

We can't go too far into psychology here, and I never did fully understand the psychological connection myself, but it does appear that a strong emotion is really a deeply connected part of your ego in some way. For example, if you should have a strong emotion that is repellent to you for some reason, and you reject it, split it off from your personality, you have a real demon in the background of your mind that is raising Cain with you to get back into contact with you.

Years ago, when I was first studying the hidden path, there was much glib talk in esoteric circles about a thing called The Dweller on the Threshold.

No one knew what it was exactly, but all spoke of it with bated breath and with great fear. I was never able to find out exactly what it is, and as time passed I forgot about it, and heard no more about it until I started practicing esoteric work.

When I had completed the preliminary work that led up to writing *The Art and Practice of Astral Projection*, I had settled many of the "conflicts." That is, I had welcomed back into me most of the things that I had formerly rejected. Therefore, when I started to project using the different systems, I encountered no Dweller on my Threshold. Oh, there were a few things as described in the book; those noises and various images came to me, but I recognized them for dream-projected images, and, as soon as I started to work with them, they disappeared (which was when I took them back into me). I will admit that I did not recognize them as projections of me, which I had formly rejected, at the time. I am just now connecting these different things so I understand them and their relation to my esoteric work.

I cannot give a course in psychology as I am not qualified to do that; nor could I do it, long distance, in this little book. But in considering this Law of E-motions I am getting close to this threshold business. This threshold business is where the emotions come in. Of course, in referring to creative visualization, I am referring to new emotions, and not to old ones, such as your projected-rejected projections would be. I am concerned that old emotions should interfere with new emotions.

Now for heaven's sake don't be suggestible, and be afraid of this work. We probably all have rejected projections to some degree in our lives. Will you do this? If you feel any deep-seated emotional upheaval when you start to do this work, or encounter an upheaval later on that you feel you cannot handle, then stop this work and go to a psychologist and ask for assistance, as you might have serious repressions that you are contacting. This does not happen very often and, in fact, I cannot think of a single case that I know of personally, but since there are so many screwballs in the world hollering about the dangers of esoteric study, I would rather warn you this way than say nothing.

The whole idea of doing esoteric study is to clear up, or resolve, the rejected parts of your personality and get them back in yourself so you can go ahead to greater things. (As I said before, I don't understand the rejection idea, and neither does anyone else, but the main idea is to get cleared up and, no matter how many different ways they say it, that is it.) Conversely if you feel only a mild upheaval, then proceed to try to handle it yourself, and go on with your work. So to proceed—

One method of using e-motions, often advocated by former creative visualization teachers of the natural type, was to instruct students to "feel" (without telling them "how" to "feel") that they already had the thing desired, and were using it, AND they would get it in due time.

This idea seems to have originally been based upon one of the few genuine portions of the New Testament.

The purported Jesus is supposed to have said, "Whatever things you want believe that you have them already and you will have them."

> Have faith in God. I tell you this: if anyone says to this mountain, "Be lifted from your place and hurled into the sea," and has no inward doubts, but believes that what he says is happening, it will be done for him. I tell you, then, whatever you ask for in prayer, believe that you have received it and it will be yours. (Mark 11:23, New English Bible)

Of course these directions are greatly simplified and are directed to people who are able to work the creative visualization laws naturally. You now know, from your study, that there are many other factors and laws that need to be taken into consideration in order to make creative visualization work. However, you now already know these other factors, and knowing them, you can use them properly, and get the best reinforced use out of all of them.

How then do you go about using the E-motion Technique Law fully? (This explanation properly belongs in the section on practice, but I will include some of it here now, and explain more later on in the practice section. We can go back to the case of the young Paris rag picker, as his story is the most simple to illustrate the principle, and the principle is the same in all cases. You remember that what the young man first worked for was a small piece of carpet to put on the floor beside his bed to protect his bare feet from the cold stone floor when he got up in the morning. He knew what the cold stone floor felt like, so he did not have to image (or visualize) the feel of THAT. Therefore from the standpoint of The Law of E-motion as applied to this rag picker, having allowed for all the other laws, the use of the Law of E-motion would consist of the young man *feeling his feet already protected by the rug under his feet, and allowing that feeling to generate the feeling-emotion of pleasure and satisfaction.* I will repeat: the feeling of pleasure of the desire fulfilled generates the emotion of happiness and satisfaction!

There is more to this E-motion work however. Let us consider E-motion in terms of another kind of an emotion we are all familiar with. Let us consider the emotion called DESIRE.

A would-be-occult-teacher once told me that this word—desire—meant *de*-of, *sire*-Father, so the word meant "of the father." This is not true, etymologically speaking, as a glance at the dictionary will show, but the idea is not a bad one to consider.

It has been argued that all desires are basic— they come from a basic cause—which can be equated with a central idea of Divinity. To take this idea further: the basic Divinity desires good for all, and implants the de-sire in all beings to cause them to reach out for this good thing that the Divinity has already created for everyone to use and to have. Certainly without desire we would all do nothing.

I trust that you can see that desire is an emotion greatly to be desired, to be cultivated, to be developed and practiced.

Naturally the best and proper practice of desire is to link it to something—something you want. You have ideas all the time about things you want, the circumstances you want brought about. And this is what you have been studying in this book. Use your Treasure Chart to the limit. Load it with pictures of things you desire and feast your eyes on them. Everything helps. The sky is the limit. Go for it. Keep in mind that you can reach for whatever is important to you. A good job, a new car, good health, good marks, creative ideas, anything that you really desire. You are in charge of yourself, so it's up to you to decide what you want.

CHAPTER 9

THE LAW OF
THE REVERSAL OF
THE PLANES

This Law of Reversal has some importance, enough that you should know about it. In actual practice it may do little more than perplex you as you go through the planes if you are viewing the effects of reversal clairvoyantly. You may have flashes of this while you are following other directions given in this book.

In case you do have a clairvoyant flash, and you notice something like a name or signpost on something, you will also notice that the words are reversed, as in a mirror. This is about the only time you will notice the reversal as the scene is not always so clear. A reversed street, for example, looks very much like an ordinary street, and it takes some examination to notice that it is reversed. This kind of close examination is not usually given in a dream scene.

Then, again, in this clairvoyant flash you may be "passing" through a plane, and by the "time" (there is actual time over there) you stop to see why the sign is reversed, you will be through that plane, and in the next plane the words will be right again.

The reason for this is: in relation to our plane the next inner plane is the reverse of this one! Then the next inner plane is reversed to that one! And so on down to the end of the planes, as far as the physical cosmos is concerned! Or to say it in a more simple way, each inner plane is inside out to each other. What is coming here is going there!

Here is a simple illustration, rather too simple in a way, but try to understand it thoroughly. Let us, for example, say that on our physical plane we plan to go for a picnic. As you well know, we would start at the beginning here, like 1–2–3–4, etc. We plan the picnic, we buy the food for the picnic, we cook the food, we pack and wrap the food, we put the food in baskets, we travel to the picnic grounds, we play all day, we eat the food, and then come back home.

Now if there were such things as picnics on the Etheric Plane (the plane next to this one) in order to "go" on a picnic you would come home first, spend the day at the picnic grounds, pack the food in baskets, prepare the food in other ways, cook the food, buy food for the picnic, plan the picnic, etc. You see that I can hardly make sense in writing this down, and yet that is the way the plane next to this plane functions.

In the section previous to this one I told you that in one of the few genuine portions of the new testament Jesus is supposed to have said, "Whatever things you want believe that you have them already and you will have them." Now, in view of this reversal process, can you see why you start out getting something by *feeling that you already have it*? By doing your creative visualization work this way, you are working with the Laws of the Inner Planes and not against them.

It can be argued that *thinking* belongs to this lower physical plane and *feeling-emotion* belongs to the next plane (whatever you are going to name the planes). So now I trust you see how you use thinking and feeling together to get what you want.

We have now come to the end of the sections devoted to the study of the Laws of the Art of Creative Visualization.

In the first part of this book, I dealt with the subject of creative visualization. Then I introduced ten different factors that I said were esoteric laws and practices that were directly connected with the art of creative visualization. I first outlined these laws and practices and then described them later in greater detail. Although I had said that I would give the practices of these laws in the latter part of the book, I did give some practices in the first part. In order to go further into how to use, practice, and illustrate these laws, I am going to have to repeat some of the things I discussed earlier.

My friends have accused me of repeating myself, and I know that I do, but I can and will say, as I have said before, this is a very difficult subject, and not easy to teach under any circumstances, especially when students are working alone, as you are, when you work from a book like this. I am not writing glorious literature that will go down in history as perfect prose for all to read and copy. No. I am writing down very difficult material about a very difficult subject. I feel that I must teach this secret knowledge and esoteric practices as exactly as it is possible to do, and in the clearest language possible. And when I think that the presentation of some obtuse subject-point is not too clear the first time, I repeat the material in another form, or in another way, or in the same way, until I feel fairly certain that the material is understood and/or could be understood by repetitive reading. I expect students to study, and to practice as many times as is necessary to master these concepts. At least you should do it if you want to understand and use the secret arts in an effective manner for the development of your true Inner Powers; to help yourself through this hard physical life and make this physical life easier.

The material that I am presenting in this book has never been given out before in this way to my knowledge. When the outlines of this material were shown to some esoteric publishers, I was urged to write three or four books, and divide up the material among those books, and not give out such new and valuable techniques in one book. However I have much more material on hand now than I will ever be able to use in my lifetime, and so you get all of it in this one book as you always will. I will hold nothing back.

I will now go over some of the ten laws again and provide additional material and practices.

The Law of Physical Visualization
For those who are not gifted with natural visualization powers, and I certainly was not, the presentation of this law, and its practice, is a Godsend. Certainly the ability to mentally visualize is absolutely necessary for creative visualization, and yet not one teacher, that I know of, has treated this matter with the importance it deserves, let alone given any directions as to how to develop visualization ability. I had to work this whole visualization matter out myself. I found that there were several ways that our mental image-making capability could be increased. I have developed several different methods of doing this.

The Technique of Physical Visualization
The second law is very closely related to the first, but I decided to divide them into two laws because the whole matter of visualization had never been treated before, and the importance of clear, mental pictures, has never been emphasized in this way before. For your first work in the practice of mental visualization you were given a ritual to learn and practice both mentally and physically. This ritual is very old and very potent when it is done right. I hope you did not neglect your work on that ritual. I gave this to you in the first part of the book so you would have something to do while you were studying the rest of the book. If you followed my directions, and did the ritual, you should have developed some marked visualization ability by now. You should be able to work the whole ritual while seated; that is, you should be able to run

over the whole ritual in your mind's eye, making all
the motions, and making all the movements back
and forth in your imagination. If you haven't done
it, then don't get discouraged, but start to do it
when you feel like it.

Working with the Symbols

Now I am going to five you some more visualization practices. You will find four black and white
symbols at the end of the book (pages 97 and
99). These same four symbols are shown in color
on the inside of the front and back covers. They
also appear on the front cover.

To keep up your work with these symbols, you
should make them yourself, first on paper and then
on parchment. Keep them very private. Keep them
protected so that other people will not see them or
have a chance to handle them. It should come
about, as you continue to use your own private
symbols, that the symbols should increase in
power, becoming successively charged with your
magnetism and the magnetism of the forces you invoke. For now, you can use the colored symbols
given in the book as visualization objects, to develop your visualization ability. (Some additional
uses were given for these symbols in my book *The
Art and Practice of Astral Projection*, and I refer you
to that book for work of an advanced nature.)

The use of the symbols for visualization practice and development is as follows. In starting the
work each time I urge you to work the ritual first,
probably physically, as you are going to do the
other work mentally, and the physical ritual will

serve as a good balance exercise. If you have time to do the ritual do it, and if you do not have time, do not do it, but do not feel guilty if you don't do it all the time.

Visualization Exercise

Start your work by making yourself comfortable. Use a table and chair of convenient size. You can have some soft music playing, but it should be definitely soft and non-stimulating, soothing and soft. Place the yellow-square-blue-border card, the card of the Element of Earth, before you, with a good light falling on the card from behind if possible. Look at the card quietly. Do not strain or force your eyes in any way, shape, or form. On the first day, look at the card for about three minutes, and then gradually increase the time to five minutes, but only one time a day. If you feel any strain, skip a day or two.

When the time interval is over, close your eyes and you will see, in your inner vision, a duplicate image of the symbol in complementary colors. Watch this image quietly and make no mental effort to interfere with it. It will grow strong and then fade away, then reappear again, each time weaker. Watch it until it is gone. Do not force any action against the image, just watch the image fade away.

Repeat this work with all the symbols, each in turn for a week each, but do not put any pressure on yourself.

After you have done this work for some weeks, then try to bring the image back into your memory, into your mind's eye. I am sure you will be pleased to discover that in about two or three weeks of work you will be able to bring the images back in your imagination vision easily—and in color!

When you reach this result, you will know that you can visualize properly if you go about it right. All that you have to do is to *look at what you want to visualize long enough to get it fixed in your memory.* (That is not what really happens; you do something quite different than merely learning to recall and visualize by just looking long enough. The looking affects the inner plane forces, but for now all you have to know is how to do it. The esoteric reasons for this belong to advanced work.)

You can now practice looking at pictures, or at real things, at things that you want, by using the same technique as given above. You have been told about Treasure Charts, and it is in the use of these charts that you can practice your visualization work extensively and profitably. Nothing is truer than the old saying, "Practice makes perfect." At least here.

. . .

Now let us consider the presentation of the concept called *The Sphere of Availability.* This concept opened up an entirely new dimension to creative visualization work. Heretofore the raw assumption of creative visualization was that anything would work if you visualized it or thought about it long enough and hard enough—and this is true—but with different people the creative process worked differently. Sometimes it worked one way and sometimes another, but it seemed to work for different people in different ways at different times!

Sometimes it seemed not to work at all. At other times, with some people, there would be long delays. For other people, short time intervals was the rule. Any of us who have tried these methods know what I am talking about. And yet there was no one to turn to. The New Thought teachers who used this law considered it blasphemy to question, in any way, any of the New Thought methods. This attitude made it very hard to get a reasonable analysis of creative visualization and its limitations, or even to work out some kind of an operating technique to explain why it did not work. Many students found creative visualization methods did not work for them, no matter what they did.

After I discovered the Sphere of Availability concept I was able to resolve many of the former difficulties that students had with creative visualization methods. The simple non-occult answer is that all people are different and, obviously, what works for one does not always work for another. People are not the same. All people are not created equal. Each person's life and resources is different from all other lives and resources.

This means that each student's approach to securing good results by means of creative visualization has to be different. We might get much better results with the creative visualization method if we were all as destitute as the Paris rag picker. The Paris rag picker was so destitute that he knew exactly what he wanted because he needed a thing like a small piece of carpet! And starting from that *exact* need he was able to build up, step by step, a Sphere of Availability that, in the end, was able to supply him with a tremendous amount of material things. I hope you will read the above over until you understand it completely.

Now we come to you and me, and our work with creative visualization. As we are not the same as the Paris rag picker in terms of our resources, *our problem is much greater than his was!* He knew exactly where he stood, and we do not know exactly where we stand. Most all of us have something. I said before that most of us are "middle class," although there is a lot of argument as to what that means. I mean that we are neither rich nor poor, but range from fairly well off to affluent. If you are normal, then you want to better yourself, you want to better your material conditions. To many of us having only a little is almost as bad as having nothing.

Your problem then is difficult, but it is not insurmountable. Using the information already given, you can restate your present problem in this way: your present sphere of availability is static. You wish to increase your sphere of availability so that it will grow to supply you with the things that you now think are necessary for your happiness and physical well being.

So the problem, now restated, becomes this: you are to find the exact point in and from which you are to construct or organize your work on your present sphere of availability. This point is just short of this side of your first desired objective.

In order to do this, you must find out exactly what your present Sphere of Availability is. You must size up your present Sphere of Availability, in a hard-headed manner, and not fool yourself by wishful thinking in any way. You are going to have to start with your present sphere of availability and build it up to the point where it will supply you with the things that you want.

Before you can start this work, there are two things that you have to know and do. You have to know exactly what it is you want to do with your life in the future. You have to know what you want to happen to you for the rest of your life, at least in general way, if not an exact way. Try writing it all down as best you can.

Now you have written down your goal, and, as you look at it, you have to understand that what you want has to come to you through your Sphere of Availability. So—now take a long hard look at your present Sphere of Availability.

Your work now becomes so personal that I cannot advise you any more about it. I will have to leave it up to you and your examination to show you where you stand. I can give you a few examples as an illustration. Let us say that your appraisal has convinced you that, for the immediate time being, your job is your Sphere of Availability. Obviously to supply you with the things you have outlined as your desired objects in life your Sphere of Availability has to be increased. Make a close examination of your job. I know this is a trite saying, but are you really working well? Are you doing the very best you can on your job? As long as you have, for the purposes of this example, decided that your job is your present Sphere of Availability, then improvement of this source supply is the start of your enlargement of your source of supply. As I said, your work with your life and your resources now becomes so personal that I cannot treat it further here.

The Law of Limitation
Let us now consider the 5th Law. Some of the practices connected with many of these esoteric laws are little more than good use of common sense, coupled with some understanding of the nature of the inner planes. The main idea we all seem to get about the inner planes is that they are free of the limitations of this physical plane, and that is true, but that freedom pertains only to the inner planes and as soon as these forces are grounded onto this plane they become subject to this plane's laws and that is what we want.

Some ideas about the actions of the forces of the inner planes can be gained from the following words of an occult writer of the turn of the century. I have in my possession of a book written by Arthur Edward Waite, published in London in 1898. In the opening chapter of his book, Mr. Waite makes the following statement about the inner planes, but, in a rather jocular mood (do not take this too seriously).

There (in the Inner Planes) all paradoxes seem to obtain actually, contradictions co-exist logically, the effect is greater than the cause and the shadow more than the substance. Therein the visible melts into the unseen, the invisible is manifested openly, motion from place to place is accomplished without traversing the intervening distance, matter passes through matter. There two straight lines may enclose a space; space has a fourth dimension, and untrodden fields beyond it; without metaphor and without evasion, the circle is mathematically squared. There life is prolonged, youth renewed, physical immortality secured. There earth becomes gold, and gold earth. There words and wishes possess creative power, thoughts are things, desire realises its object. There . . . the hierarchies of extramundane intelligence are within easy communication. . . . There the Law of Continuity is suspended by the interference of the higher Law of Fantasia.*

As I said, Mr. Waite was speaking rather jokingly, but the above statements do give some ideas of the differences that are considered to be so between the inner planes and this one.

For the purposes of your work in creative visualization, the main idea to remember is that inner plane forces are not subject to any kind of lower physical plane form of confinement until they are grounded in some way. Once grounded in and on the physical plane they are then confined and cribbed so you can handle them.

In the mental magic type of work you will be doing you can easily gather the inner plane forces, but they fly off in all directions at once just as

---

* A. E. Waite, *The Book of Ceremonial Magic* (London: Wiliam Rider & Son, 1911, originally issued in 1898), pp. 3–4.

easily. However, there is a way you can hold them. For the purposes of the simple work you are doing it will be sufficient if you conduct these forces into a *form* and the form will be your visualized picture object form.

Or, if you will make a declaration before starting your creative visualization work, it will usually be sufficient to bind the forces to the extent of the particular operation you are performing. Try to get into the habit of writing down beforehand what you want to accomplish. Put a definite end to each separate section of the work you are doing. Do not run all your creative visualization work together with no end in sight. Split up your desire-work in sections and work to get one section done at a time, completing each section and closing off that section. These procedures will act very effectively as binders of the inner plane forces that you "capture" for your work.

Keep in mind the stories I told you about the misers who got money started toward them and then could not spend the money for anything when they got it—not even for food—and ended up starving to death. This is more or less common when a person has creatively visualized for money instead of for things or circumstances. Try to do your visualization work for things and circumstances, and not just for money. If you visualize for money, you could get it and then not be able to use it for the things you want. Even ordinary events can keep you from using the money for what you wanted it for.

I once had a peculiar experience along these lines. I am writing this book on an IBM typewriter.

Ever since I was aware of this typewriter I wanted to own one. I did not do any real visualizing work to get one because my Sphere of Availability was just about able to supply one. The work I did was to find the best second-hand typewriter that I could for the best price. I worked myself into quite a pitch doing this and it became a sort of enjoyable game (which is another thing you want to incorporate into your work—make it fun). I ran across one in Hollywood and I almost bought it, but I didn't quite like it, and the price was higher than I felt I could pay. After some thought about the matter, I decided to let it go. However on my next trip to Los Angeles I did find a splendid typewriter with an extra long carriage, which is what I really wanted, at a price very close to what I had decided I would pay. Now, however, I still find myself looking at the papers and looking at prices for typewriters. I still have a feeling for buying a typewriter, and I have two now! In my case the feeling is not too strong, but it is there, and if it ran away with me, it could make trouble. I could end up buying typewriters without needing them. I might even buy some more typewriters at a very good price and resell them at a profit, which is an acceptable course to follow. So watch out for the continuation of your desire feelings after the desire has been filled. Turn it to something else as quick as you can.

The Law of Binding
Our physical cosmos is governed by polarity much more than we realize. In fact, being able to realize the polarity of the physical cosmos, and being able

to recognize it, is an art of illumination. For Heaven's sake look about you from now on and take the dual nature of the Universe into account. For Heaven's sake remember that what goes up must come down. It takes a well-developed person to recognize polarity, and a still more well-developed person to take advantage of it. Even such a mundane thing as the stock market shows this effect very clearly. When the stock market goes up, the less developed person is attracted by that effect and is drawn into the rising market. When the market goes down, that person is deeply discouraged by that fact and gets out. People follow effects and do not note the causes. I cannot remember the name of the very rich man who said frankly that the reason he was so wealthy was that he bought when everybody was selling and sold when everybody was buying. Of course no one believed him and went on just as they were doing.

The point of all this is that all forces that influence the physical plane are dual—they have two sides. Every force that you contact to do work for you has this double sidedness to it, and when you contact the force, you contact both sides at once.

Now although you may get the force to work for you the way you want it to work for some time, the time will come, sooner or later, when the opposite side of the force will take over and you will, by its reversal, lose all you have gained! And that often happens when you least expect it.

How can you protect yourself from this reversal effect due to the dual nature of all forces? In your creative visualization work it will probably be sufficient if, keeping the dual nature of all forces in mind, you add, when you write down your limitation statement, a further statement that goes something like this: "I also desire that when the object of this particular creative visualization work has been attained that no reversal take place, but that the opposing force of the force that I am invoking be bound, and that I possess the object gained as long as I can use it profitably and successfully." It might be well to also make the statement to the effect that, "I am to possess the object gained until it can be replaced with a better object, etc." Most any statement like that will act as a binding.

Almost any statement like the above will be all right to use as long as you use it with common sense and mean it. It is not the possible powerlessness of any binding action that you might take that makes the trouble. It is the ignorance of the existence of the reaction of dual forces, or that all forces are dual, that makes the trouble.

One of the most outstanding cases I ever heard of concerning the ignorance of this dual nature of forces is the case of Mrs. Eddy, the discoverer and founder of the Christian Science Church, to whom every believer in metaphysics must be grateful for her pioneer work along these lines. It has been said that during the latter years of Mrs. Eddy's life, she suffered from strange attacks at night, during which she suffered acutely with great distress. No one has ever diagnosed these attacks correctly. Mrs. Eddy referred to them as Malicious Animal Magnetism. I feel rather certain that these strange attacks were due to the "other" side of the forces she invoked, and taught others to invoke, without binding the other side of the force. Everything points to that being true. The malicious animal magnetism could have been the unbound side of the force called divine love which she invoked so much. I mean no disrespect to Mrs. Eddy and I do not want to start any argument about this. I regard Mrs. Eddy with great respect and I give her full credit for the great work she accomplished.

The Law of the Barrier

Words and emotions are twin tools that you use in creative visualization work. You should be well-equipped in words and well equipped in emotions for creative visualization work! However if you have only a few words at your command that is still all right, as long as those few words are connected with strong emotions. It is the strong emotions that do the inner plane work and not so much words. A strong emotion of desire is very necessary for this work. Many people are afraid to allow themselves to feel strong emotions of desire. And yet it is desire that is the driving force of our lives. Without desire we are nothing. Many people, when they lose their desire to live, actually lie down and die without more ado about it.

When you use the next law, use desire for all it is worth. If you feel your emotional desires should be whipped up a bit, then, as long as you recognize it for what it is, do a little daydreaming in connection with your Treasure Chart. Find pictures that give you a "thrill" and play on and intensify that thrill.

The Law of the Treasure Chart

One pretty good teacher I know teaches that you should construct dramas of events that you want to take place. You can use this device very well in connection with the pictures that you put on your Treasure Chart. Arrange the pictures so that they tell some kind of a story. Use your ingenuity to construct a sequence of picture stories which will bring about the desired thing or circumstances that you desire. Do not be too concerned with gaps in the pictures, but supply your own imagination bridges to cross the gaps. The main idea is to whip up your desire emotions so that they produce an effect on your subconsciousness.

In carrying out these dreams let yourself go. Make the characters in the pictures say and do what you want them to do. However you had better not picture actual persons, that you know, doing these things. Real persons are apt to feel your work, and the feeling will set up currents of opposition to your proposals. Work only with imaginary people and imaginary pictures of things, or real pictures of things but imaginary pictures of people. What you are doing is working with the counterparts of the real things, and you can have a large degree of control over the counterparts that you cannot have over real people and/or things. The counterparts are far easier to control than the physical things they represent, and much can be done in working with them. So do not work with real people as it can be very unsatisfactory in your results, not that it is "wikkid," just unsatisfactory.

The Law of E-motions

As is usual in this work, The Law of E-motions goes on over into the next law to come, the reversal law. All these laws are pretty well connected, especially when we get into these fine spun distinctions as we are doing now. Here is another definition of E-motion. An emotion is a thing that is of the nature of now-ness. There can be no such thing as a future emotion. All emotions are now!!! You can have an emotion about a thing that you think might come to you in the future but the emotion you have is right now! You cannot think of an emotion without having it!

The previous reasoning is the basis for working with emotions. Another way you can look at it is this: as the next plane to this is reversed to this one, you can regard it as a sort of mirror and you can see in that mirror the things that you already want. Suppose you come up to that plane as you do to a mirror on this plane, and you hold up something that you want to that plane-mirror (in your imagination). Well there is the thing you want visible on that reversed-inner-plane-mirror! And being as it exists there now, by your work of visualizing it there, the means of its existence on that inner plane had to come into being, too, just had to, or you could not even see it in your mind picture there! Therefore, by your creation of the imagination image, you brought the means of its existence into being! And the reason you can do this is because of the reversed nature of the plane next to this plane "above."

Now look! If you do not get too far off the beam by daydreaming, you can, in fantasy, trace back a possible line of creation of the mirrored object and then when you get back far enough, you can attempt to link that fantasy line with your sphere of availability!!

You can try this. I guess it won't hurt as long as you keep your perspective! Use any sort of thinking, feeling, fantasy, daydreaming, planning, researching whatever it is that suits your nature. Feel free to experiment all you please, and do it freely, keeping in mind that you are daydreaming and you know it, but remember that back of it all lies your Sphere of Availability in reality.

Here at this point we could go off the deep end and start talking about atoms, elemental forces, are things really real? What does real really mean? But we must be practical. You can say that the intense emotions that you generate throws out streamers of a drawing force that draws the things desired to you, and this must be true because you usually get the thing that you "emote" for. (Of course in this day and age of multiplied manufacturing processes we actually do not have to get one certain thing, a duplicate of that thing will surely do. So try to keep this idea in mind, leave it open.) But one thing is certain. You do have to have the desire which in turn created the emotion created by the desire.

Actually the way I am stating this is all wrong. The way it sounds is that you do not work on your Sphere of Availability unless you want something and then you turn it on. That is wrong. I did not mean to give that idea at all. Your life should be a planned growth of your Sphere of Availability with all in order and no wild side trips as I seem to be advocating. In fact, so natural should your building of your Sphere of Availability become that you sort of forget about it as you go about doing it.

Remember (I again repeat) the object of your life should be to build up your Sphere of Availability so that it can bring you the things you want, and what you want should be what you set your goal for; and to set your goal you should do some serious thinking and planning.

If what you want is a Rolls-Royce, then you must remember that to get a Rolls-Royce you must have a Rolls-Royce type of Sphere of Availability, and until you do have it, you won't get the car. However, there is one positive thing you can say and that is this: through successive steps of building properly, correctly, and perfectly—and a few other things—you can build up your Sphere of Availability so you can reach the Rolls-Royce type of Sphere of Availability supply base! I do not think anyone will argue against that.

IN CONCLUSION

I am reading over these pages and I wonder: did I leave anything out? What obvious thing should I have said? I could have written better prose. But if I don't stop, I can go on endlessly improving the words and sentences, revising, revising, revising—endlessly—and if I did that, I don't know when I would ever get through with a book at all.

I will cover/hedge by saying, as I said in my first book, I am not trying to write glorious prose—I will never be a great writer/author—no, I am writing only to teach basic esoteric knowledge and basic working directions. I write about a very difficult subject, perhaps the most difficult subject in the whole world, the subject of human beings and their powers, and how we can use them to protect ourselves from the hurts of the physical plane. Certainly this is a subject that staggers our ability and confidence. I write not to help myself, not to help you, but to teach you to help yourself!!!

I have been expecting to be accused of writing too few pages on such a large subject. I must admit that I did not pad out the pages of this book. I tried very hard to go right to the core or heart of the secret teachings, and, in as simple language as possible, to explain the basic knowledge of the art of getting material things through creative visualization. I then laid out the tools of the trade, followed by practical working directions for using the tools. I tried to keep things clear and to the point, not going to much into rapturous new thought gush about divine love as opposed to cold intellectualism, for neither extreme will get us anywhere. I write for earnest, average, students—so you can understand the material and use it. So for heaven's sake, and for your own sake, learn the art of creative visualization, and use it!!

—OPHIEL

INDEX

About The Author

Ophiel was one of America's best known teachers of esoteric study. He didn't follow any "school" of thought, but studied every tradition, distilling information, and making it available to people who wanted to start to learn about secret traditions, or who wanted to work with Extra Sensory Phenomena. His Art and Practice series (including *The Art and Practice of Creative Visualization, The Art and Practice of Astral Projection, The Art and Practice of the Occult, The Art and Practice of Talismanic Magic, The Art and Practice of Cabala*) is probably one of the most practical sets of instructions ever written for beginning students. His work has received rave reviews from many teachers who started their study with Ophiel's books. Ophiel taught classes and worked with readers by mail, while living in the state of California. He retired to San Francisco, where he died from heart failure on August 17, 1988 at the age of 84.

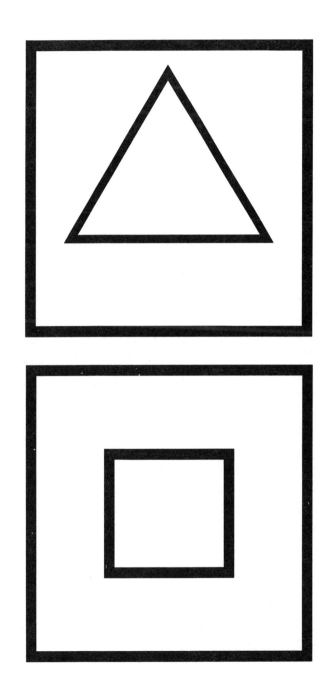

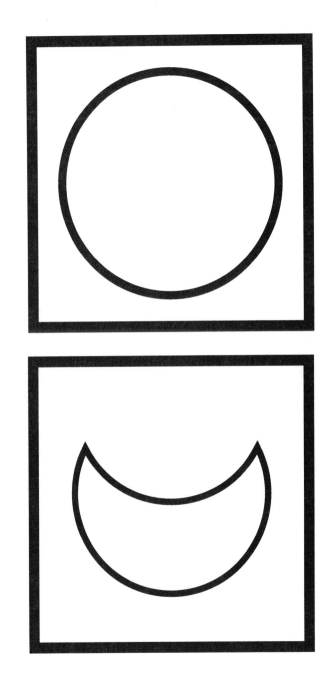